Invitations to Personal Reading
Curriculum Foundation Classroom Library
Scott, Foresman and Company

Books to Read Aloud

The Big Golden Book of Poetry	edited by Jane Werner
Finders Keepers	Will and Nicolas
Little Frightened Tiger	Golden MacDonald
The Man Who Didn't Wash His Dishes	Phyllis Krasilovsky
The Old Woman and Her Pig	illustrated by Paul Galdone
Rosa-Too-Little	Sue Felt
Six Foolish Fishermen	retold by Benjamin Elkin
The Three Billy Goats Gruff	P. C. Asbjørnsen and J. E. Moe
Umbrella	Taro Yashima
Where Does the Butterfly Go When It Rains	May Garelick

Books to Enrich the Content Fields

The Big Book of Real Fire Engines	illustrated by George Zaffo
The Listening Walk	Paul Showers
One Snail and Me	Emilie McLeod
The Sky Was Blue	Charlotte Zolotow
What Is A Turtle	Gene Darby

Books for Independent Reading

Belling the Cat and Other Stories	retold by Leland Jacobs
Big Talk	Miriam Schlein
Cowboy Small	Lois Lenski
Gertie the Duck	Nicholas Georgiady and Louis Romano
Indian Two Feet and His Horse	Margaret Friskey
Josie and the Snow	Helen Buckley
Karen's Opposites	A. and M. Provensen
Millions and Millions and Millions!	Louis Slobodkin
Nothing but Cats, Cats, Cats	Grace Skaar
Robins and Rabbits	John Hawkinson

The
Listening
Walk

The
Listening

Special Scott, Foresman and Company Edition
for the *Invitations to Personal Reading* Program

Walk

by PAUL SHOWERS

illustrated by ALIKI

THOMAS Y. CROWELL COMPANY   New York

This edition is printed and distributed by Scott, Foresman and Company by special arrangement with Thomas Y. Crowell Company, 201 Park Avenue South, New York, N. Y. 10003.

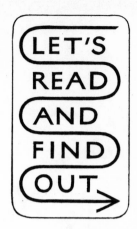

The
Listening
Walk

I like to take walks.

I take walks with my father and our dog.

Our dog is called Major.

He is an old dog and he does not walk very fast.

We go down the street and we do not talk.
My father puffs his pipe and thinks.
Major walks ahead and sniffs.
I keep still and listen.

I call this a Listening Walk.
On a Listening Walk I do not talk.
I listen to all the different sounds.
I hear many different sounds when I do not talk.

First I hear Major's toenails on the sidewalk.
Major is an old dog. He has long toenails.
When he walks, his toenails scratch the sidewalk.

They go *twick* *twick* *twick* *twick*.

I hear my father's shoes on the sidewalk.
My father walks slowly and his shoes go *dop* *dup* *dop* *dup*.

I can't hear my shoes. I wear sneakers.

I hear all sorts of sounds on a Listening Walk.
I listen to sounds I never listened to before.
I listen to lawn mowers.
Lawn mowers are noisy.

A power mower has a motor.
The motor makes a steady zooming noise.
It goes like this:

z-z-z-z-zzzzzzooooooooooooooooommmm.

A lawn mower that you push makes a different noise.
It goes

ratch   atch   atch   atch   atch.

If you push it faster, it makes more noise.
Like this:

ratch-atch-atch-atch-atch.

I like to listen to lawn sprinklers.
Lawn sprinklers are very quiet.
They make different sounds.
Some sprinklers make a steady whispering sound.
Like this:

thhhhhhhhhhhhhhhhhhh.

Other sprinklers turn around and around.
They go like this:

whithhhhh   *whithhhhh*   *whithhhhh*   *whithhhhh*.

On a Listening Walk I hear cars in the street.

The shiny new cars are quiet.
They make only a soft *hmmmmmmmmmmmmmm*.

But old cars are very noisy.
Old cars sound like this:

rackety rack

rackety rack   rackety rack.

When cars stop quickly, the brakes go *eeeeeeeeeeeeeeeeeeee*.

When cars go around the corner too fast,

the tires go *whhrrrrrrrrrrrr.*

On a Listening Walk I hear all kinds of sounds.

A baby crying:

waaaa   awaaaa   awaaaa   awaaaa.

A bicycle bell ringing:
trrring   trrring.

A boy goes by on roller skates.
His skates go

rak

rawk

rak

rawk.

A lady hurries by us.
She is wearing high heels.
The lady's high heels go
    bik
       bok
         bik
           bok.

A bus is coming.
The lady starts to run:
    bik
       bik
         bik
           bik.

The bus stops at the corner:
pfsssssssss.
The lady gets on.

The bus starts up again:
chrrrooooooooff.

Sometimes my father and I take Major to the park.

I like it in the park.

It is cool and shady.

It is quiet there until a jet flies over.

Jets are very noisy. A jet goes

eeeeeeeyowwwoooooooooooooo.

In the park my father and Major and I walk down the shady path.
I like to listen for sounds in the park.
They are not loud sounds like the noises in the street.
I have to keep very quiet to hear them.

We walk along the dirt path under the trees.
I do not talk. I listen.
I listen to my father's shoes on the path.
They make a soft sound. They go

chuff

      chuff

           chuff

                chuff.

I listen to the birds in the park.
I listen to the pigeons and the ducks.
The pigeons fly down to meet us.
They want us to feed them.

The pigeons puff up their feathers.
They take little, tiny steps.
They come toward us, nodding their heads.
They say

prrrooo

prrrooo   *prrrooo.*

prrrooo

At the pond the ducks are waiting.

They want us to feed them, too.

The small ducks swim up close.

They turn their heads on one side and look at us.

The small ducks waggle their tails and quack.

The small ducks say

gank gank

wonk wonk

gank gank.

The big ducks are not so brave.

They stay back and swim around in circles.

The big ducks look at us but they do not come close.

The big ducks say

gaaaaank   gaaaaank   gaaaaank.

I like it in the park.

I hear many different sounds there.

I listen to the birds.

I hear the ducks and the pigeons.

Sometimes I hear a woodpecker.

The woodpecker sounds like a little hammer.

He goes

rat-tat-tat-tat-tat-tat.

I hear many sounds in the park.

I hear crickets in the grass.

They go

creet   creet   creet.

I hear the wind in the leaves.
It whispers

shhhhhhhhhhh.

I hear bees in the flowers:

bzzzzzzzzzzzzzzzzzzzzzzzzzzzzzzzzzzzzz.

It is fun to go on a Listening Walk.
You do not have to go far.
You can walk around the block and listen.

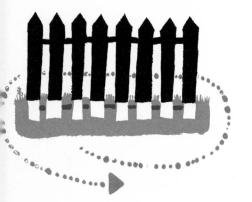

You can walk around your yard and listen.

You do not even have to take a walk to hear sounds.
There are sounds everywhere all the time.
All you have to do is to keep still and listen to them.
Right now there are sounds you can hear.

When you finish this page, close the book and listen.
How many sounds can you hear right now?
Close your book and count the sounds you can hear.

RIGHT NOW.

ABOUT THE AUTHOR

PAUL SHOWERS is a newspaperman who also does free-lance writing. Starting out as a copy editor first on the *Detroit Free Press* and then the *New York Herald Tribune*, he spent the war years as a sergeant on the staff of *Yank*, the army weekly. Subsequently he worked briefly for the *New York Sunday Mirror* and then joined the staff of *The New York Times*, where he is now assistant travel editor. Besides writing occasional stories for the *Times* Travel Section, he is the author of a play which was produced some seasons ago at the Pasadena Playhouse in California.

Born in Sunnyside, Washington, Mr. Showers grew up in various parts of the country: a suburb of Chicago, Muskegon, Michigan, and Rochester, New York. With his wife and two children, he now lives in Leonia, New Jersey, where he rates himself as a "very amateur gardener."

ABOUT THE ARTIST

ALIKI BRANDENBERG was born in New Jersey and grew up in Philadelphia, Pennsylvania, where she attended the Museum College of Art. She has traveled extensively throughout Europe, and for four years she lived and worked as an artist in Switzerland.

Now the Brandenbergs live in New York City, where Mrs. Brandenberg does free-lance artwork and is especially busy illustrating books for children.